GREETINGS FROM
Vera B. Williams
STORY AND PICTURES

and Jennifer Williams
MORE PICTURES

STRINGBEAN'S TRIP TO THE SHINING SEA

GREENWILLOW BOOKS *An Imprint of HarperCollinsPublishers*

Stringbean's Trip to the Shining Sea
Copyright © 1988 by Vera B. Williams and
Jennifer Williams
All rights reserved.
For information address
HarperCollins Children's
Books, a division of HarperCollins
Publishers, 10 East 53rd Street,
New York, NY 10022.
Manufactured in China
www.harperchildrens.com

Various materials were used to create

the postcards, including watercolors,
Magic Markers, and colored pencils.
Library of Congress Cataloging-in-Publication Data
Williams, Vera B.
Stringbean's trip to the shining sea.
Summary: Stringbean describes his trip
to the west coast in a series of postcards.
[1. Postcards—Fiction. 2. Travel—Fiction. 3. West (U.S.)—Fiction.]
I. Williams, Jennifer. II. Title. PZ7.W6685St 1988   [E]   86-29502
ISBN 0-688-07161-9 ISBN 0-688-07162-7 (lib. bdg.)
ISBN 0-688-16701-2 (pbk.)

First Edition 09 10 11 12 13 SCP 10 9 8

POST CARD

Dear Readers,

Here are the postcards and snap-shots that Stringbean Coe and his brother Fred sent home to their mother, their father, and their grand-father. They're from the long trip Stringbean made one summer with Fred in Fred's truck with the little house built on the back.

Their grandfather made this album for the family.

Love Vera, Jenny, and the people at Greenwillow Books

ARTIST: VERA B. WILLIAMS

NAMES & PLACES

THIS SPACE FOR ADDRESS

Readers

Planet Earth

The Solar System

The Universe

POSTCARD

Dear Ma, Pa, Grandpa and Potato,

We didn't even get started right after we said goodbye to you. We stopped to buy me a hat like Fred's. Then we had to stop at Moe's junkyard for an extra spare tire.

I hope the photos you took with Grandpa's old camera turn out. You'll see the truck looks really great - not like a piece of Junk like you said.

You know what Mr Moe even said to Freddy? "I'll buy that Truck back from you for a good price". My brother is not nuts. He told Mr. Moe no way and that this was an important trip we had to take.

Mr Moe gave me a pretty postcard he had saved from a long time ago. I'll send it too.

love Stringbean

GRANDPA, I PROMISE TO TAKE PERFECT CARE OF YOUR CAMERA.

COE FAMILY

THIS SPACE FOR ADDRESS

COE SPRINGS MOTEL

JELOWAY, KS.

66708

P.S. Grandpa tell Potato I miss her a lot. But don't let her bark loud at Fred's rabbit like she does when she gets mad at us.

S.

FRED

STRINGBEAN'S SCHOOL
PHOTO

THE MORNING BEFORE THEY LEFT
[OUTSIDE FRED'S GARAGE]

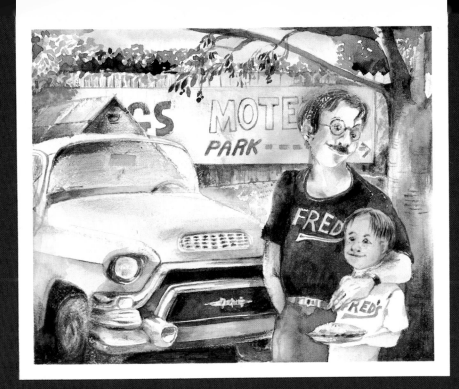

POTATO JUST AFTER
STRINGBEAN LEFT. SHE
WOULDN'T GET UP OR
EAT OR DO ANYTHING.
↓

THE TRUCK WITH THE HOUSE FRED AND STRINGBEAN
BUILT ON THE BACK. STRINGBEAN IS HOLDING THE PIE
WE BAKED THEM FOR A SEND-OFF. HE CLIMBED UP
AND PICKED ALL THE CHERRIES OFF OUR TREE
THE DAY BEFORE THEY LEFT.

Greetings from the Pacific Ocean

MESSAGE HERE

Dear Ma, Pa and Grandpa

Mr. Moe saved this card from a trip he took a long time ago.

He liked the idea we were going all the way to the Pacific ocean. I showed him the map in the road atlas you gave us.

"That's the ticket" he said to me. "The Pacific ocean.. Yes. You'll be driving along one day and you'll come through some hills and redwood trees and there she'll be.....THE PACIFIC OCEAN, one of the shining seas, the biggest one too."

He told me to say hello to the seals on the beach for old Mr. Moe. I promised I would.

love
Stringbean

my signature is → → →
getting good like yours Grandpa

ARTIST: JENNIFER WILLIAMS

SEVEN SEAS CARD CO.

THIS SPACE FOR ADDRESS

Coe Family
Coe Springs Motel
Jeloway, Ks.
66708

Dear Folks,
Please give Lily carrots with her rabbit food. And don't worry about us. Stringbean still doesn't eat much but we're having a great time already.

love
Fred

CHICKADEE

CROW

BLUEBIRD

DUCK

SPARROW

HAWK

WOODPECKER

OWL

GOLDFINCH

CARDINAL

BOBWHITE

ROBIN

BIRDS

ORIOLE

DOVE

Mrs. Rose Jones with the great willow that shelters the birds who summer here.

❧ POST CARD ❧

Dear Ma, Pa and Grandpa,

We are sending photos to prove Potato
is O.K. and just fine after looking for us
the whole night.

Freddy says he was so excited when he
phoned you he's not sure he told you just
where she found us. Well it was here. Isn't
she smart?

We were swimming in this lake by a
big old willow tree. You know how Potato
doesn't like water but she came right on in
and landed right on top of me with a big
SPLASH. The birds in the willow all flew out.
I <u>KNEW</u> she wouldn't stay home without
me.

love from Stringbean and
Potato X xxxx
↗ a big dog kiss

ARTIST: JENNIFER WILLIAMS

NATURE CARDS SERIES #2—BIRDS

Dear Folks,
Stringbean is
<u>utterly</u> and
<u>completely</u> and
<u>totally</u> happy
now. He made a list of
special places we should see
while I made a sketch for you.

ADDRESS

MR. and MS. COE
and MR. F.M.
COE SPRINGS MOTEL
JELOWAY, KS.
66708

P.S. I am going to get Potato
a hat like mine and Fred's.

COOLER

DISH STORAGE

PROPANE STOVE

FOOD STORAGE

SKETCH OF BACK OF TRUCK — thought you'd like to see my drawing of our wonderful kitchen.

love Fred

This sod house was built in 1871 by Mrs. Lovey Johnson. The first midwife to practice her profession in this area, summer and winter she rode her pinto over the prairie to help at births. She lived on this spot till she was one hundred years old. Many a child was named for Lovey Johnson by grateful parents.

LOVEY
ANDREWS

LOVEY
TUCKER

MRS. LOVEY JOHNSON,
MIDWIFE

JOHNSON
PETERSON

Dear Ma, Pa and Grandpa,

We stopped to see what this place was. It's very old. It's a history place. We watched the shadows of the clouds go over.

I think the clouds here are the ghosts [good ghosts] of those people the midwife helped to get born. I think they are looking after her little empty old house.

love from me (Stringbean)

Dear Folks,

This was the first time Stringbean stopped talking since we left Jeloway! I guess you did warn me.

Driving away from this special old place it got so dark and poured so much we had to stop. Water to the hubcaps! We curled up in our house in the back and ate peanuts and listened to the radio.

love Fred

P.S. We are thinking up a name for the truck.

Do you like HARRY-THE-CHARIOT or WINNIE-THE-WHEEL?

S---n-b--n

★ CREATED BY VERA B. WILLIAMS ★ LUCKY HISTORY CARDS ★

ADDRESS

The COE FAMILY
COE SPRINGS
MOTEL
JELOWAY, KS.
66708

PPS. DO YOU LIKE MY LETTERING? Maybe I will be a sign painter someday.

W U.S.A.
5 A.M.

LAZY RIVER CAMPGROUND

EASILY REACHED FROM MANY ROADS, WE HAVE PLENTY OF WATER, HAY, AND SHADE TREES. THIS IS A FAVORITE STOPPING PLACE FOR TRAVELING CIRCUSES. EARLY-RISING CAMPERS ARE OFTEN REWARDED BY THE SIGHT OF A CIRCUS ON ITS WAY AT DAWN.

Dear Ma, Pa and Grandpa,

We stayed in the exact same campground as the circus.!! ☆*,*:

We got here in the dark. Potato and me were asleep already. But in the morning I was looking out at a big old elephant. [really]. But we only got to see them packing up and moving out with thier thur stuff. It was so early there were still stars up in the sky.

After when I was looking around around I found one of the clown's great big shoes! I hope they have extras. Freddy says we'll catch up to them so we can give it back. It's a big

funny shoe. I think it's a lucky shoe. Potato loves this shoe!
love Stringbean

INTERNATIONAL SOMERSAULT GAMES U.S.A.

W

ARTIST: JENNIFER WILLIAMS

PUT YOUR BUSINESS ON A CARD

□ □ □ □ THIS SPACE FOR ADDRESS □ □ □ □

COE FAMILY

COE SPRINGS MOTEL

JELOWAY, KS,

66708

P.S. We are going to stay at a Buffalo Ranch tomorrow tonight. I am excited. . This isn't such good printing because I did it too fast.

AMERICAN BISON, or BUFFALO

Before hunting made them extinct in the wild, buffalo roamed the plains of the U.S. and Canada by the millions. Cow or Buffalo Birds flew around them and slept in the wool of their manes at night.

Dear Ma,

Remember I cried that time you told me too much hunting had killed off almost every buffalo. NOW THERE ARE BUFFALO AGAIN.

One reason is Mr. Harlee Hawkins. He started this ranch with just 4 wild buffalo. Now there are 200. He is a Sioux. His grandma told him how once buffalo used to cross the river for 6 days and 6 nights. And there were so many passenger pigeons it made the sky dark. There were so many eagles. There were so many elk.

Mr. Hawkins says the exact same thing grandpa says, "Well kid that was then. This is now."

I love the way buffalos have curls growing down their noses. Ask aunt Tina for me, "Would you like if a buffalo came to your beauty parlor for a shampoo?"

love and hugs x x x x x x

ARTIST: JENNIFER WILLIAMS

NATURE CARDS SERIES #1—ANIMALS

Dear Folks,

I hope Lily is doing well. I'm wishing for a big litter.

Love Fred

FAVORITE SHOES

W   U.S.A.

THE COE FAMILY

COE SPRINGS MOTEL

JELOWAY, KS.

66708

P.S.

So far no trouble with truck. Stringbean checks the oil and tires so don't worry.

x x Stringbean

F.

ANSWER ▷ FOOTHILLS ⛰

TAKE A BREATH BEFORE YOU START CLIMBING.
CAMP AT **FOOTHILLS REST.**
FOLLOW THE GREEN ARROWS FROM THE HIGHWAY.

Dear Ma, Pa, Grandpas,
See, that place marked with an X ?
That's where we're going to stay tonight.
It's a foothill. They just stick up all of a
sudden like Potato under the covers.
These are the first mountains I was ever
in (on ? in ?).

   Fred says we'll come to mountains
where the snow never melts. We'll be able
to see all over, (maybe we'll get to even see
where those circus trucks went to.) We are
going to stop and see the town where
Grandpa used to be a silver miner.
~~and~~ We're going to climb up and see
the oldest trees in the world. Then
we have to cross the desert.

P.S. Potato likes to bark to the coyotes in
the dark. I'm learning names of stars.
We roasted corn in our fire. It's very good that way.

VERA B. WILLIAMS

THE ODDBALL CARD CO.

US A
Mary Marshall Brownie
Founder,
United Dogs
of Canada
& the U.S.
W

THIS SPACE FOR ADDRESS

COE FAMILY

COE SPRINGS MOTEL

JELOWAY, KS

66708

love, Stringbean

Did you know there is a star named
BETELGEUSE ?

POST CARD

Bears are not pets. Do not feed them or approach the cubs. Place all food out of bears' reach.

WHAT DID THE BEAR SEE WHEN SHE WENT OVER THE MOUNTAIN?

more and more and more mountains. We saw bears swimming! Really we did.

These mountains are really high. I looked way way down. I saw a car upside down in a creek. Freddy drove so slow around and around the curves. I beeped the horn.

Today we hiked to the top. So far this is the best place. Eagles live up here. I'm going to be a mt. climber, so is Potato.   love Stringbean

Dear Folks,
Those bears were close! Stringbean fell over holding onto Potato so she wouldn't

go after them. We stood back and made a lot of noise. We sure weren't easy till they swam away.
Love
Fred

USA   USA

HOT-AIR BALLOON
W   INVENTED 1783

~ THIS SPACE FOR ADDRESS ~

COE FAMILY

COE SPRINGS MOTEL

JELOWAY, KS.

66708

how is LILY ?

P.S. I hope I will see a Rocky Mt. Bighorn Sheep.

NATURE CARDS   SERIES #1—ANIMALS——ARTIST: JENNIFER WILLIAMS

JOSEFINA VALDEZ MULLER

Boarding house prop. Fed entire town during great blizzard

FREDERICK MULLER

Miner Organized union of silver miners

ANDREW McKAY

Mine carpenter Built mine support system following great cave-in

DR. EMILY CASTLETON

Physician Founded town's first hospital

MISS ROSE BROWN

Publisher and printer of town's first weekly, *The Silver Dollar Gazette*

MRS. LETTY SOREN AND DAUGHTER MAY

Started first general store on Main Street

NAMES UNKNOWN

Children employed at mine shed

ELY FLASHTAIL

Muleteer and hero of the big cave-in

RON BABCOCK

Millwright and inventor

JOHN TENG

Miner

BONITA LIVESY

Dairy woman and farmer

Visit this graveyard of white stones. It honors miners and their families who trekked here from far places to build a once-famous and busy town in these mountains.

This and other history cards for sale at the new museum on Mill Street, formerly a boarding house owned and run by Josefina Valdez Muller.

Post Card

Grandpa, your old house is a museum now and they have cards with pictures of your parents on them!

Dear Grandpa (I'm going to try cursive)
We came out of the long long tunnel and it was just like you said. We saw the big old rock crusher on the hill and the broken down houses.
We went everywhere you told us about. They even let you go down in the old mine. We rode on the train that used to take out the silver rocks. I rode with the driver. The shed where you worked when you were a kid is still there. It has a big hole in the roof.
We picked lots of little flowers to put on the graves for great grandmother Josefina and great grandfather Frederick.
love from your Grandson,
Stringbean Cesar Joseph Coe

P.S. I owe you that quarter Grandpa. The 3 Giants Mts. really do turn purple at sunset.

USA
W
FAVORITE TOOLS

THIS SPACE FOR ADDRESS

MR. FREDERICK MULLER

c/o COE SPRINGS MOTEL

JELOWAY, KS. 66708

P.P.S. Grandpa,
How come you never said all those stories you told us were real History. WOW! K.

The town is now a ghost town, but the canyon is well worth a visit.
In late spring over one hundred waterfalls have been counted.

THIS SPACE FOR MESSAGE

Dear Ma, Do you believe in GHOSTS?

A man where we stopped to look at rock specimens told us about this canyon. He gave me this card and said we should watch for the ghost horse.

Freddy didn't even want to come here. We had a big *argument. Then he was glad we came. But only because of the waterfalls. We got so hot and our mouths got full of dust driving down the mountains.

Fred says there is no such thing as a ghost but in the night I saw something cloudy moving along the rocks. And I did hear hoof beats.

* Fred and me have some BIG fights. He only likes history places and fishing and cars. Potato

likes the same things I like. Potato and me miss you.
love and kisses xxx
Stringbean

DESIGNED AND PAINTED FOR FRIENDS OF GHOST TOWNS BY JENNIFER WILLIAMS

THIS SPACE FOR ADDRESS

Ms ELENA COE
my mother →
COE SPRINGS MOTEL
JELOWAY, KS. 66708

Dear Folks,
That son of yours, Stringbean sure is stubborn. I guess he takes after Grandpa...... AND
HAPPY BIRTHDAY TO YOU GRANDPA ON YOUR 82nd. I'll Call you —
Lots of love Fred

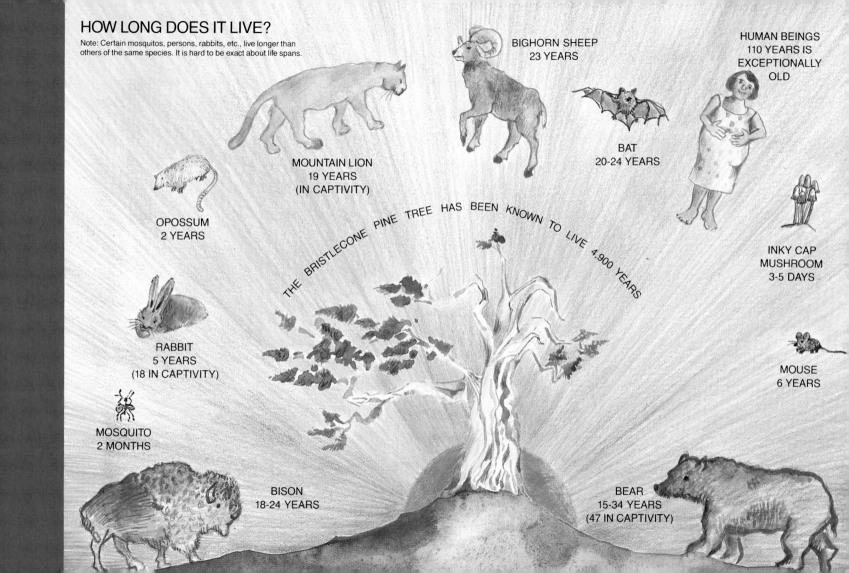

HOW LONG DOES IT LIVE?

Note: Certain mosquitos, persons, rabbits, etc., live longer than others of the same species. It is hard to be exact about life spans.

BIGHORN SHEEP
23 YEARS

HUMAN BEINGS
110 YEARS IS
EXCEPTIONALLY
OLD

BAT
20-24 YEARS

MOUNTAIN LION
19 YEARS
(IN CAPTIVITY)

OPOSSUM
2 YEARS

THE BRISTLECONE PINE TREE HAS BEEN KNOWN TO LIVE 4,900 YEARS

INKY CAP
MUSHROOM
3-5 DAYS

RABBIT
5 YEARS
(18 IN CAPTIVITY)

MOUSE
6 YEARS

MOSQUITO
2 MONTHS

BISON
18-24 YEARS

BEAR
15-34 YEARS
(47 IN CAPTIVITY)

BRISTLECONE PINE TREES ARE BELIEVED TO LIVE LONGER THAN
THE MEMBERS OF ANY OTHER PLANT OR ANIMAL SPECIES ON EARTH.
THE RINGS ON ONE TREE HAVE SHOWN IT TO BE 4,900 YEARS OLD.

POST CARD   POST CARD

HAPPY BIRTHDAY GRANDPA

Do you like this card? We went to see the
oldest living things in the whole world.
They are trees called Bristlecone Pine trees,
They are much older than you Grandpa.
One of them might need 4900 candles.
The wind blows so much up here these
trees grow all twisted like corkscrews.
It snowed here. It was hot when we start-
ed up. I didn't have my jacket. I froze.
But POTATO loved it. She chased snowflakes.

NATURE CARDS SERIES #3— BIOLOGY FACTS COURTESY OF THE NEW YORK PUBLIC LIBRARY / ARTIST: VERA B. WILLIAMS

she should live
up here in summer.
Only she might come
out all twisty too.

love Stringbean
your best grandson

USA
THE GREAT
TRICYCLE
RACE
USA   W

Mr. F. Muller

COE SPRINGS

MOTEL
JELOWAY, KS

66708

BEST LITTLE BIG STORE IN THESE MOUNTAINS. WE HAVE EVERYTHING. AND THEN SOME
MORE. THINGS OLD, THINGS NEW, RED, GREEN, YELLOW, BLUE. WHATEVER YOUR
POCKETBOOK, WHATEVER YOUR FACE . . . COME RIGHT IN AND TRY THIS PLACE.

**ARMSTRONG
& DAVILA**

LITTLE BIG STORES

* ARTIST: JENNIFER WILLIAMS

* PUT YOUR BUSINESS ON A CARD

Hi Folks,
Stopped at this nice store to get a new
lure I want to try. And new running shoes
for Stringbean. His toes are growing right
out his shoes. (They'll get to the Pacific
before we do.)
And would you believe it?. The salesperson
says to Stringbean," you know just ½ hour
ago there was a real circus clown sitting in that
chair trying on our biggest shoes. But he only wanted to buy one." Stringbean's eyes bugged out!
He ran and got the clown's shoe. He described
the circus trucks to the woman. "That's them,"
she said.
I grabbed Stringbean (his face in a big
chocolate ice cream cone) and we drove all over town looking. No luck.
We've been calling them the Mystery Circus.

* Freddy bought
* me such great shoes
* and he let me take
as long as I wanted
to decide.
love S.

Coe Family
Coe Springs Motel
Jeloway, Ks.
66708

...love F

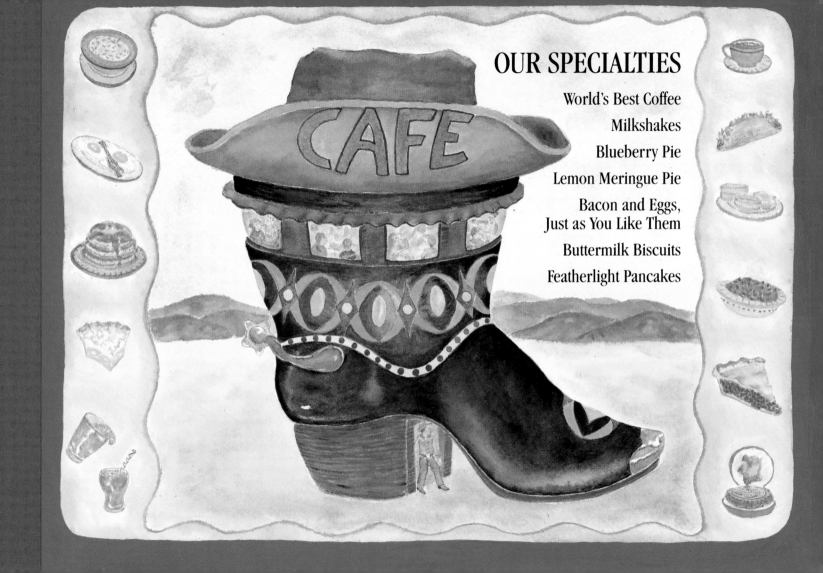

OUR SPECIALTIES

World's Best Coffee

Milkshakes

Blueberry Pie

Lemon Meringue Pie

Bacon and Eggs,
Just as You Like Them

Buttermilk Biscuits

Featherlight Pancakes

BOOT CAFE
THE ONLY ONE OF ITS KIND IN
THE WORLD. GOOD EATING RIGHT
ON THE EDGE OF THE DESERT.

POST CARD

Dear Ma,

Don't you wish this place could be near Jeloway? We are worried about our money lasting. Fred says we shouldn't eat in any restaurants. But I never ate inside a **BOOT** before.

Tomorrow we cross the desert. Freddy says we need to start so early it won't even be light out. Freddy thinks of lots of important things. But he's too bossy. We made this pact for crossing the desert.

PACT

Fred promises not to tease and boss and Stringbean promises hot to talk and talk all the time and not to <u>whine</u>

Cesar J. Coe

Fred Coe

FAVORITE PIG-OUT   U.S.A.

P.S I do <u>not</u> talk all the time. I don't talk in my sleep but Fred snores ~~~.

ARTIST: JENNIFER WILLIAMS

PUT YOUR BUSINESS ON A CARD

ELENA M. COE

THE BEST **COE SPRINGS MOTEL**

JELOWAY, KS.

66708

MANY FASCINATING SPECIES OF LIZARD CAN BE FOUND IN THE SOUTHWESTERN U.S. HORNED LIZARDS OR HORNED TOADS, FOR INSTANCE, LOOK LIKE MINIATURE DINOSAURS. THEY BURROW IN THE SAND AT NIGHT, CAN ALTER THEIR COLORING, AND WHEN EXCITED SPURT BLOOD FROM THEIR EYES.

Dear Mapa and Grandpa,

At last we saw the circus trucks on the road up ahead of us. Fred said it could be a mirage. But he was kidding. (Anyway a mirage looks like water.)

We were really catching up with them this time. Then you know what happened? One of our tires blew. ☆ Harry went zigzag all across the road till Freddy could stop her.

But guess who changed the tire? Your son Cesar Stringbean J. Coe changed the tire. Only Freddy had to help get the bolts off. And it was so hot we had to get our potholders to hold the tools. But meanwhile we lost the circus again.

Stringbean

☆ Remember we named the truck HARRY-THE-CHARIOT

ARTIST: JENNIFER WILLIAMS — ANIMALS — SERIES #1 — NATURE CARDS

HAULING MELONS — IN THE 1920s
USA
W

Coe Family
Coe Springs Motel
Jeloway Ks.
66708

P.S. But we found a new pet. It's just like the one on the card.
PPS. It's stringbean's pet not mine.
How come you raised a kid who can't let anything that crawls go by without adopting it?
Potato hates this heat. She envies Lily at home in the shade. How's Lily?
love to all of you back there

FUTURE PRESIDENTS USA

USPS MESSAGE CARD

Dear Post Office →TO MY ᴼᵂᴺ MOTHER
please deliver
COE SPRINGS MOTEL
JELOWAY, KS.
66708

DEAR MA,

   I MISS YOU. AND DADDY TOO.

   I MISS GRANDPA TOO. I MISS LILY TOO.

   THE OCEAN IS STILL FAR AWAY.

   FRED IS **VERY** MEAN.

   He made me let my lizard go.

                love Stringbean

P.S. I have given up on finding that clown and giving back his shoe.

TRAIN TRESTLE CAMPGROUND

A DRAMATIC SITE WHERE ROCKY MT. BIGHORN SHEEP SHOW THEMSELVES HIGH ABOVE THE TRESTLE. THIS TRAIN TRESTLE IS A FAMOUS EXAMPLE OF THE CONSTRUCTION FEATS OF RAILROAD AND BRIDGE CREWS WHO LAID THE TRAIN TRACKS ACROSS RIVERS AND SWAMPS, OVER MOUNTAINS AND DESERTS, FROM THE ATLANTIC TO THE PACIFIC OCEAN.

Dear Folks,

MADE IT ACROSS THE DESERT O.K!

Spending 2 whole days in this great campground. Washed all our stuff, washed Harry-the-Chariot, patched my Jeans.

I'm worried about money. Might need to ask you to wire some.

Stringbean found some kids to play with. What a relief! Sending photos.

love, Fred

P.S. I don't hate Freddy anymore. He even lent his good fishing rod to my friends.

P.P.S. We didn't catch a single fish.

ARTIST: VERA B. WILLIAMS

GREAT CONSTRUCTION PROJECTS

P.P.P.S. But we found a snake. (Potato found it really.)

P.P.P.P.S. My friends are going to keep the snake.

P.P.P.P.P.S. We let that snake go.

COE FAMILY

COE SPRINGS MOTEL
JELOWAY, KS.
66708

JANIS AND JEANNIE'S

WORK WITH NATURE AND SHE'LL WORK WITH YOU is our motto.

Be sure to stop and try our produce.

Dear Folks,

They needed some extra pickers at a big strawberry farm down the road from this stand.

Stringbean saw the kids who pick with their families so he thought it would be fun. Ha ha. Its a hard way to make not much money. They pay by the box and we were pitiful. Stringbean got so tired he even wanted to go home! He sure ate a lot of berries too.

By the way, you won't recognize little brother. Can't see his ribs anymore. He eats! You should have seen the size of those potatoes we baked last night, Grandpa!

ARTIST: JENNIFER WILLIAMS

P.S.
I never said I wanted to go home. Only Potato didn't like being tied up while we picked strawberries all day.

COE FAMILY
COE SPRINGS MOTEL
JELOWAY, KS.
66708

AND ANYWAY----→ NOW WE ARE ONLY 300 MILES FROM THE PACIFIC OCEAN

Tomorrow we drive straight there. I promised Fred, NO STOPS.

love, J.

Greetings from
the Pacific

THE PACIFIC OCEAN—
63,801,668 SQUARE MILES, THE LARGEST OF THE OCEANS.
LONG MAY IT CONTINUE AS HOME TO THE SEAL, THE WHALE, AND THE SALMON.

Dear Everybody,

Stringbean Cesar Joseph Coe from the Coe ~~Stringbean~~ Springs Motel in Jeloway, Ks. is sitting on a rock with his feet in the PACIFIC OCEAN writing you this postcard.

Ma, remember the ocean was in my dream and you said maybe I would be disappointed when I saw it for real. Well I just want to tell you that I am not even one little bit disappointed.

And Potato just loves the beach. You should see that dog chase waves.

Love Stringbean

PS We drove right through a giant redwood tree on the way to this beach. Fire made a tunnel through it a long time ago.

ARTIST: JENNIFER WILLIAMS

FACTS ABOUT OUR PLANET CARDS

AMBER WAVES OF GRAIN

W U S A

Dear Postman, Please take this card 1500 miles to the

COE SPRINGS MOTEL JELOWAY, KS. 66708

RIGHT IN

"I DID FIND THEM!"

I really always knew I would. And they were right on the same beach with us. Only They were camped way down at the other end.

Potato and me saw Their camp when we climbed up on the hill To watch for Seals.

Now I am friends with the clown. He has a name that you can read backwards too. OTTO. He was so glad to get his Shoe back. I can't exactly explain but he says each clown has very, very

Special shoes just for that clown and no other clown has the same ones. S.

COE FAMILY

COE SPRINGS MOTEL

JELOWAY, KS. 66708

Dear Folks,
Stringbean is having the best time here. Potato is jealous of S's new friends.
see you soon Fred

STRINGBEAN AND SOME FRIENDS HE WENT FISHING WITH AT TRAIN TRESTLE CAMPGROUND. [His friends' mother took this photo especially for Stringbean to send us.]

OTTO THE CLOWN KINDLY SENT US THESE PHOTOS. STRINGBEAN SAYING HELLO [AND GOODBYE] TO THE SEALS FOR MR. MOE.

STRINGBEAN IN CLOWN MAKE-UP AND OTTO'S TIE. SOME CLOWN!!

Dear Ma, Pa, and Grandpa,
   My name is not Stringbean
anymore. Yesterday I changed it back
to Cesar. I'm not even a little
bit skinny now so I can't be
Stringbean anymore.
   I helped water the elephants
this morning. I wish I could always
live on the beach with the circus!
But I would miss you and all my
friends too.
   **THIS IS THE LAST POSTCARD I AM GOING
TO SEND. I'M TIRED OF WRITING CARDS**
and Fred is going to drive back to
Jeloway fast.
   But wasn't I good? I did send one
every day like I promised....Did you
save them all like you promised?
   your son and grandson
      Cesar

ARTIST: VERA B. WILLIAMS

PLANETS, STARS, AND SPACE

USA
W
CLOWNS

COE FAMILY
COE SPRINGS MOTEL
JELOWAY, KANSAS
66108

POST OFFICE   Thanks for taking all these
              cards to my house.

(P.S) There are still 4 oceans and lots of
seas I haven't even ever seen !